A Coloring & Activity

Max & Ruby

Valentine's Day Fun!

Grosset & Dunlap

Based upon the animated series *Max & Ruby*
A Nelvana Limited production © 2002–2003.

The publisher does not have any control over and does not assume any responsibility for author or third-party websites or their content.

Published in 2008 by Grosset & Dunlap, a division of Penguin Young Readers Group, 345 Hudson Street, New York, New York 10014. GROSSET & DUNLAP is a trademark of Penguin Group (USA) Inc. Manufactured in China.

ISBN 978-0-448-44981-4   1 0 9 8 7 6

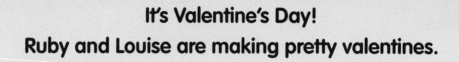

It's Valentine's Day!
Ruby and Louise are making pretty valentines.

Look at Ruby's colorful valentine!
Color Louise's valentine to match Ruby's valentine.

Max is having trouble sorting the shapes that Ruby cut out. See if you can help. Use the key below to color the shapes.

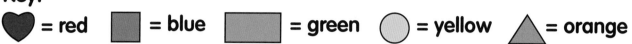

Key:
♥ = red   ■ = blue   ▬ = green   ○ = yellow   ▲ = orange

Now Max needs to count how many of each shape he has.
Draw lines to match.

1
2
3
4
5

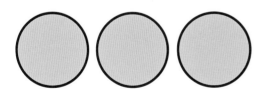

Max is playing with his fire engine since he's too little to use scissors to cut out valentines.

Use these steps to draw a fire engine.

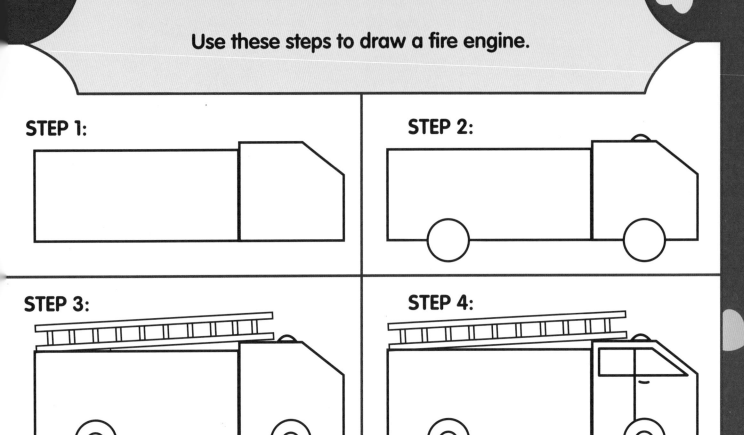

STEP 1:

STEP 2:

STEP 3:

STEP 4:

Draw your fire engine below.

Color all the pictures that have to do with Valentine's Day in red.

BE MINE

Max makes a special valentine for Grandma.

Color the two pictures that are the same in each row.

Candy hearts are the perfect Valentine's Day treat!
Help Max count the hearts and then trace the number.
Write the number on your own, too.

Create your own special valentine.

Happy Valentine's Day!

Max is a bunny who likes balls and boats.
Bunny, balls, and boats all begin with the same sound.
Color things that begin like bunny in blue.

Max needs to take all the valentines to the mailbox.
Can you help him find his way?

START

FINISH

Happy Valentine's Day from Max, Ruby, and Grandma!

ANSWERS:

Page 4:

Page 5:
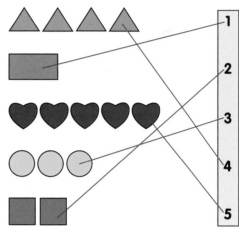

Page 8:

Page 10:

Page 13:

Page 14:
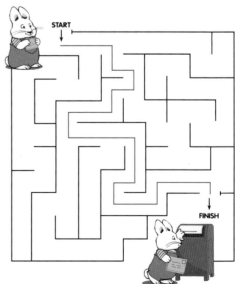